THE BUNYIP OF BERKELEY'S CREEK

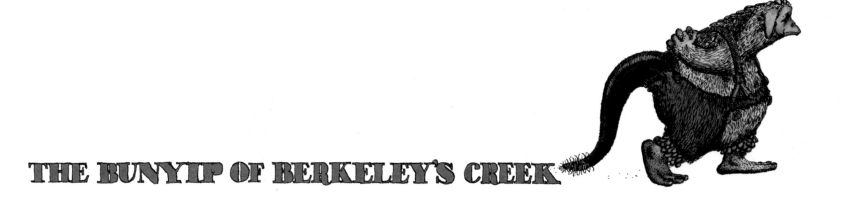

THE BUNYIP of BERKELEY'S CREEK

Story by Jenny Wagner
Pictures by Ron Brooks

PUFFIN BOOKS
in association with Childerset

Late one night, for no particular reason, something stirred
in the black mud at the bottom of Berkeley's Creek.

The fish swam away in fright,

And the night birds in the trees hid their heads under their wings.

When they looked again, something very large and very muddy was sitting on the bank.

"What am I?" it murmured. "What am I, what am I, what am I?" And the night birds quickly hid their heads under their wings again.

In the morning the thing was still sitting there,
scraping the mud off itself to see what was underneath.

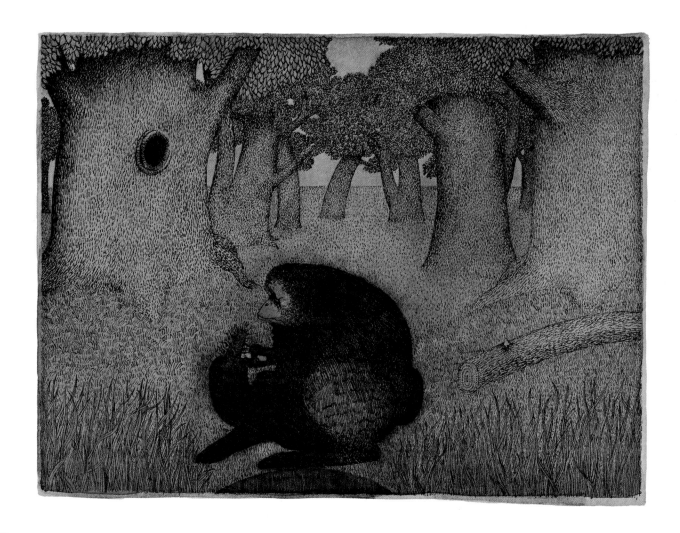

"What am I?" it kept saying. "What am I?"
But the night birds were all asleep.

A passing platypus solved the problem. "You are a bunyip," he said.

"Bunyip," murmured the bunyip contentedly. "Bunyip."
Then he sat up straight and called out, "What do I look like?"

But the platypus had dived into the creek.
"Am I handsome?" called the bunyip. "Am I?"

But nobody answered him, and the bunyip went on sitting there
for a long time, lost in thought.

Presently a wallaby came by to drink at the creek.
"What do bunyips look like?" asked the bunyip.
"Horrible," said the wallaby. "They have webbed feet, and feathers."

"Fine, handsome feathers," said the bunyip hopefully.
"Horrible feathers," said the wallaby firmly,
and finished her drink and hopped off.

"Handsome webbed feet?" called the bunyip,
but there was no answer.
The bunyip sighed and walked off to find someone else.

There was a rustling in the bushes behind him, and suddenly an emu shot past.
"Wait!" called the bunyip, running after him.
"What do bunyips look like?"

The emu stopped and considered.
"They have fur," he said at last, "and tails."
"How many tails?" asked the bunyip.
"One to each bunyip," replied the emu.
"Fine, handsome tails," said the bunyip.
"Horrible tails," said the emu. "And even more horrible fur."
And he settled his feathers and crouched down low,
and streaked off into the distance.

The bunyip wandered sadly along the creek. "Will someone tell me what bunyips look like?" he said, to anyone who would listen.

But there was no answer.

Further along the creek he met a man.

The man was busy with a notebook and pencil,
and did not look at the bunyip.
"Sh," he said, "I'm busy."
The bunyip waited for a long time,
and then he said, very slowly and clearly,
"Can you please tell me what bunyips look like?"
"Yes," said the man, without looking up.
"Bunyips don't look like anything."
"Like nothing?" said the bunyip.
"Like nothing at all," said the man.
"Are you sure?" said the bunyip.
"Quite sure," said the man, and looked right through him.
"Bunyips simply don't exist."

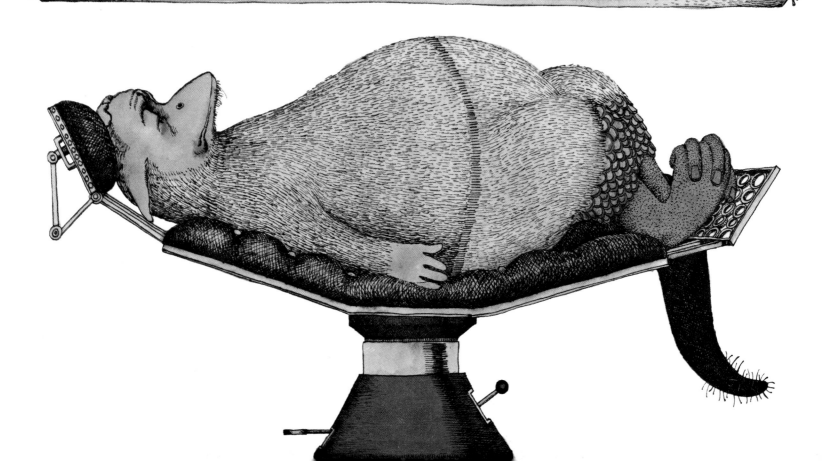

The bunyip was shaken. Then he sighed a long, deep sigh.
"What a pity," he murmured. "What a pity, what a pity."
And he walked slowly back to his waterhole.

Then he fished his belongings out of the water,
packed them in his bunyip bag, and walked away.
No one saw him go.

The bunyip walked all day, and just as the sun was setting
he came to a quiet, still billabong.

"This will do," said the bunyip to himself. "No one can see me here. I can be as handsome as I like."

And he unpacked his bag, and laid his bunyip comb and mirror out on the sand, and put his billy on to boil.

No one saw him and no one spoke to him.

But late that night, for no particular reason, something stirred in the black mud at the bottom of the billabong.

The bunyip put his comb down in surprise, and stared. Something very large and very muddy was sitting on the bank.

"What am I?" it murmured. "What am I, what am I?"

The bunyip jumped up in delight. "You are a bunyip!" he shouted.
"Am I? Am I really?" asked the other bunyip; and then,
"What do I look like?"

"You look just like me," said the bunyip happily.

And he lent her his mirror to prove it.